06

26

Sophie's Window

Holly Keller

Greenwillow Books
An Imprint of HarperCollins Publishers

Sophie's Window

Copyright © 2005 by Holly Keller

All rights reserved. Manufactured in China.

www.harperchildrens.com

Watercolors and black line were used to prepare the full-color art.

The text type is Cooper.

Library of Congress Cataloging-in-Publication Data

Sophie's window / by Holly Keller.

"Greenwillow Books."

p. cm.

Summary: When Caruso, a little bird who is afraid to fly, is blown

out of his home one windy night, he must rely on a new friend, a

dog named Sophie, to take him back to his parents.

ISBN 0-06-056282-X (trade). ISBN 0-06-056283-8 (lib. bdg.)

[1. Birds—Fiction. 2. Dogs—Fiction. 3. Friendship—Fiction.

4. Fear—Fiction.] I. Title.

PZ7.K28132 So 2005 [E]—dc22 2004042355

First Edition 10 9 8 7 6 5 4 3 2 1

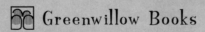 Greenwillow Books

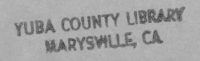

For Corey and Craig

"The sky is so big," Caruso said.
"Do I have to do it today?"
"No," Mama said,
"but you'll have to do it soon."
"Don't think so much about it," said Papa.

But Caruso couldn't stop thinking about flying.

What if he got lost in a cloud?

What if he got
tired and
fell?

Splat!

"Maybe tomorrow," said Mama.

"Maybe tomorrow," said Papa.

"Maybe tomorrow," said Caruso.

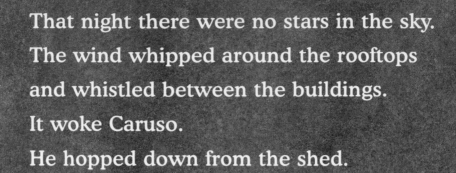

That night there were no stars in the sky.
The wind whipped around the rooftops
and whistled between the buildings.
It woke Caruso.
He hopped down from the shed.

Suddenly a big gust howled across the roof
and curled around him.
"Help!" Caruso shouted, but nobody could hear him.

Caruso went up and up and up.
Then, *whoosh,*
he went down, down, down.
When he landed,
he didn't know where he was.

In the morning, big black eyes
were looking at him.
"Hello," the dog said. "I'm Sophie."
Caruso thought Sophie looked friendly,
but he couldn't be sure.
"I'm Caruso," he said in a very soft voice.

"Make yourself comfortable," said Sophie. "It's a very nice day."

"Thank you," said Caruso, "but I want to go home."

He pointed to a yellow building with a small shed on its top.

"There it is," he said. "That's where I live."

"Well, maybe I'll see you another time," said Sophie,
and she pulled her nose inside.

"Wait," said Caruso. "I can't fly."

"Then how did you get here?" Sophie asked.

Caruso told her about the wind.

"Maybe I could just give you a little push,"
Sophie suggested.

"Oh, no," said Caruso.

"So-o-ophie, breakfast."

Sophie's ears perked up.

"This *is* a dilemma," she said.

"Good luck, Caruso."

And she disappeared.

"I see you're still here," said Sophie
when she finally came back.
She gave Caruso a piece of toast.

"We'll have to think of something
to do with you," she said, "because
you certainly can't stay."

Caruso sighed.

"I suppose I can take you home," said Sophie.

"How will you find it?" Caruso asked.

"A dog knows the streets," Sophie said.

"A bird is supposed to know the sky," Caruso said,
"but I'm not sure if I ever will."

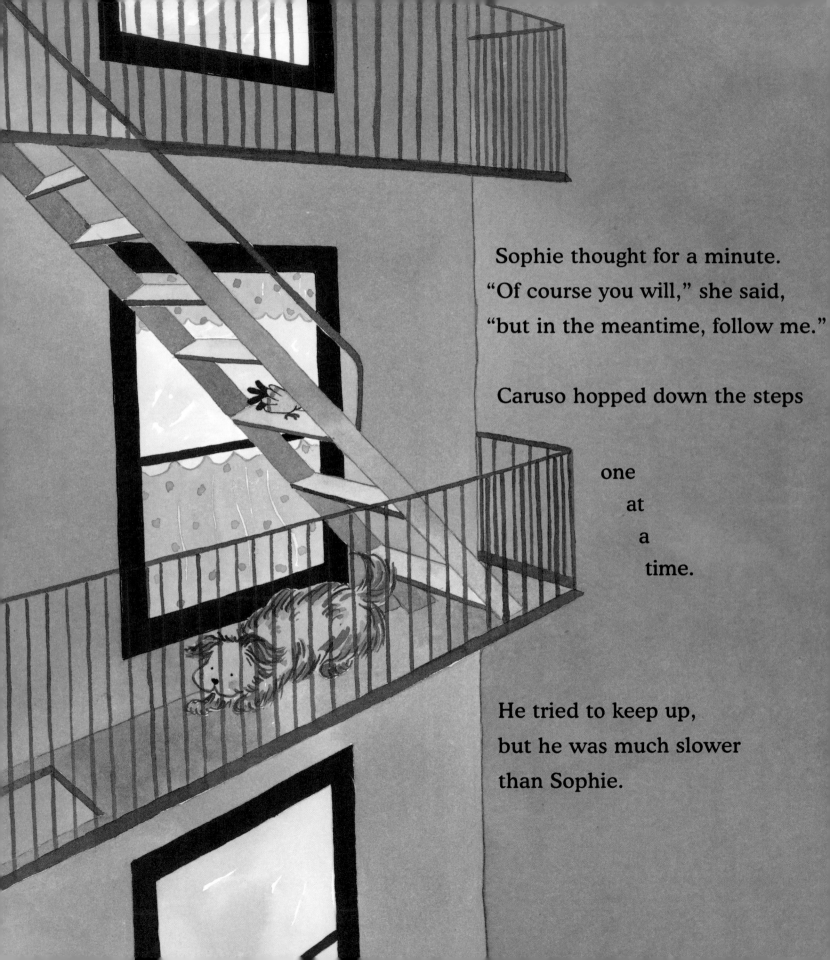

Sophie thought for a minute.
"Of course you will," she said,
"but in the meantime, follow me."

Caruso hopped down the steps

one
at
a
time.

He tried to keep up,
but he was much slower
than Sophie.

When Caruso finally reached the sidewalk,
Sophie had disappeared from sight.
"This isn't going to work," she said,
reappearing from behind a trash can.
"We'll never get you home at this rate."

Sophie lay down on the sidewalk
and Caruso hopped onto her back.
His heart was beating fast.

Sophie went up and down curbs

and around corners.

She went into a building

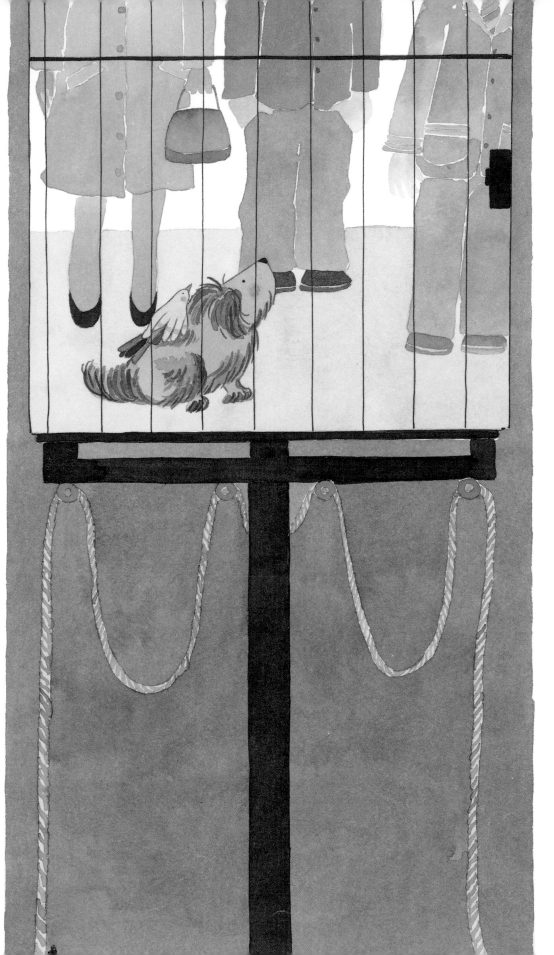

and through a gate,
which was
quickly closed
behind them.
Caruso heard a
clank and a
screech.
He felt his stomach
lurch.

Then the gate opened again.
Sophie bumped Caruso off her back
and gave him a push.
"Last stop," she said.

In a minute Caruso was surrounded by
Mama and Papa.
He tried to explain what had happened.
When he got to the part about Sophie,
he turned to find her,
but Sophie was gone.

Days and nights went by.

Caruso couldn't stop thinking about Sophie.

What if he never saw her again?

One morning Caruso opened his eyes
and knew that he was going to do it.
He climbed up onto the top of the shed,
stood on the tips of his feet, and flapped his wings.
Nothing happened.

He flapped harder.
Then harder and faster and harder and . . .

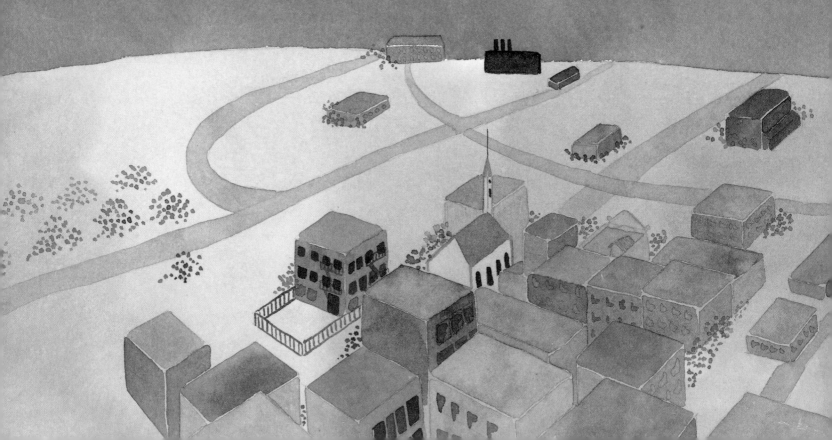

He was flying!

Sophie barked happily when she saw him.
"I *knew* you would come," she said.

They talked and played together all day.

"Will you come back tomorrow?"
Sophie asked when it was time
for Caruso to go home.
"I will," Caruso promised.
And Sophie watched until
he was just a small speck
in the sky.